What Does the Rabbit Say?

What Does the Rabbit Say?

Jacque Hall

ILLUSTRATED BY
Reg Cartwright

A DOUBLEDAY BOOK FOR YOUNG READERS

A Doubleday Book for Young Readers
Published by
Random House, Inc.
1540 Broadway
New York, New York 10036
Doubleday and the portrayal of an anchor with a dolphin are trademarks of
Random House, Inc.
Text copyright © 2000 by Jacque Hall
Illustrations copyright © 2000 by Reg Cartwright

Library of Congress Cataloging-in-Publication Data
Hall, Jacque.
    What does the rabbit say? / by Jacque Hall ; illustrated by Reg Cartwright.
    p. cm.
    SUMMARY: Rhyming text presents the sounds made by various animals, from
quacking ducks to buzzing bees, and wonders what the rabbit says.
    ISBN 0-385-32552-5
    [1. Animal sounds—Fiction. 2. Rabbits—Fiction. 3. Stories in rhyme.] I. Cartwright,
Reg, ill. II. Title.
    PZ8.3.H1445 Wh 2000
    [E]—dc21
                                      98-44375
                                           CIP
                                           AC

The text of this book is set in 26-point Maiandra.
Book design by Trish P. Watts
Manufactured in the United States of America
March 2000
10 9 8 7 6 5 4 3 2 1

To Dale, who would have been so proud . . .
—J.H.

For Benjamin Henry
—R.C.

Ducks quack. Cows moo.

Chickens cluck. Doves coo.

Monkeys chatter as they play.

But what does the rabbit say?

Pigs oink. Owls hoot.

Geese always honk and toot.

Frogs croak on the pond all day.

But what does the rabbit say?

Dogs bark. Sheep say "Baaaa."

Snakes hiss. Goats say "Maaaa."

Bears growl and donkeys bray.

But what does the rabbit say?

Lions roar. Parrots squawk.

Turkeys gobble. Horses neigh.

But what does the rabbit say?

Coyotes howl at the moon.

Birds sing a special tune.

Bees buzz by the hive all day.

But what does the rabbit say?

Rabbit hops.

Rabbit jumps.

Rabbit's feet go
thump, thump, thump!

Rabbit makes no peep or call.

And still we love him best of all!